Moon Pops

by Heena Baek

Owlkids

It was a very, very hot night
in the middle of summer.
It was much too hot.
Too hot to sleep.
Too hot to do anything.

Everybody turned on their
air conditioners, *whir-whir*.
They turned on their fans,
rattle-rattle.
They opened their fridge
doors, *hum-hum*.
And they closed their
windows to the heat, hoping
to finally get some sleep.

Drip

.

.

.

.

.

Drip

.

.

.

Drip

What was that sound?

The moon was melting!

Granny ran out from apartment 503 with a bucket to catch the falling moon drops.

"What do I do with this?" she wondered.
An idea popped into her head.
A moon-pop idea.
Granny mixed a recipe for a frozen treat.
She poured in the melted moon,
saving a few final drops.

The air
conditioners
whirred,
the fans rattled,
the fridges
hummed.

Uh-oh!

All the whirring and rattling and humming
had caused a power outage!
Everybody stepped outside.
It was almost too dark to see.

One bright light glowed from apartment 503.
Everyone followed the light to Granny's door.

Granny stepped out to greet her neighbors
with frozen moon pops.
She handed them out, one by one.

They were icy and sweet.

As everyone licked their
moon pops, something
strange began to happen.

The heat was melting away.

Back home in their beds, everyone slept with their fans and air conditioners turned off, their fridge doors shut tight, and their windows open wide. Their dreams were icy and sweet.

Knock,
knock,
knock.

.

.

.

Who could it be now?

Granny welcomed two strange rabbits into her home.
She felt she had seen them somewhere before.

"We come from the moon," they told her.
"Our home has melted away."

"Oh, how terrible." Granny sat and wondered what to do.
Her eyes fell on an empty flowerpot sitting on the kitchen table.

Suddenly, an idea sprouted.
A moon-sprout idea.
She poured the last of the
moon drops into the pot.

Sure enough, an evening
primrose bloomed.
It grew big, bright, and round
like the moon.
The petals opened to the
night sky.

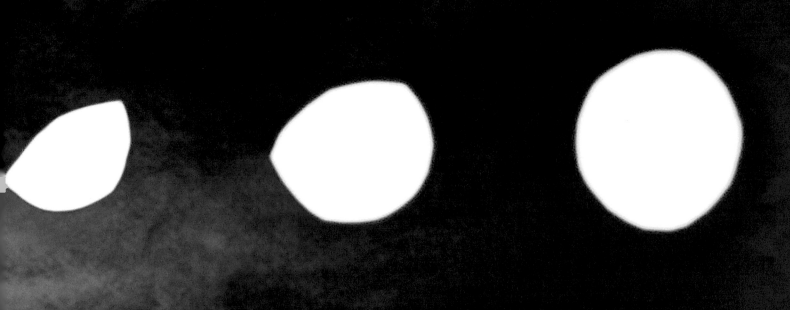

Granny and the rabbits waited.
A small spot of light sprouted
from the flower, lifting high up
into the darkness.
It grew
bigger,
brighter,
rounder...
into a full moon.

The rabbits cheered and danced
back up to their home in the sky

At last, Granny got into bed.
She wished for dreams that were
icy and sweet.

"Good night, everyone."

Owlkids Books acknowledges the financial support of the Canada Council for the Arts, the Ontario Arts Council, the Government of Canada through the Canada Book Fund (CBF) and the Government of Ontario through the Ontario Creates Book Initiative for our publishing activities.

Published in Canada by
Owlkids Books Inc.
1 Eglinton Avenue East
Toronto, ON M4P 3A1

Published in the United States by
Owlkids Books Inc.
1700 Fourth Street
Berkeley, CA 94710

Library of Congress Control Number: 2021931022

Library and Archives Canada Cataloguing in Publication

Title: Moon pops / by Heena Baek.
Other titles: Dal sha-bet. English
Names: Paek, Hŭi-na, author, illustrator. | Kiaer, Jieun, translator.
Description: Translation of: Dal sha-bet. | Translated by Jieun Kiaer.
Identifiers: Canadiana 20210110163 | ISBN 9781771474290 (hardcover)
Classification: LCC PZ7.1.P34 Mo 2021 | DDC j895.73/5—dc23

Manufactured in Shenzhen, Guangdong, China in March 2021 by WKT Co. Ltd.
Job #20CB2368

A   B   C   D   E   F   G

 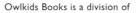

Publisher of Chirp, Chickadee and OWL
www.owlkidsbooks.com | Owlkids Books is a division of bayard canada